**FLYER books are for confident readers
who can take on the challenge of
a longer story.**

Can YOU spot the aeroplane
hidden in the story?

For Finn

A former teacher, EOIN COLFER is now a full-time writer, working from his home in Wexford where he lives with his wife Jackie and children. His other books include two more Ed Cooper stories – *Ed's Funny Feet* and *Ed's Bed* – as well as bestselling novels for older readers – *Benny and Omar*, *Benny and Babe* and *The Wish List*. Eoin has achieved worldwide success as the author of the *Artemis Fowl* books.

WOODY has been an illustrator for eighteen years, specialising in children's books and anything funny. He loves animals and nature and lives in Devon with his mate Windsor – a rather large tabby cat!

Going potty

Eoin Colfer

Illustrated by Woody

THE O'BRIEN PRESS
DUBLIN

First published 1999 by The O'Brien Press Ltd,
12 Terenure Road East, Rathgar, Dublin 6, Ireland.
Tel: +353 1 4923333; Fax: +353 1 4922777
E-mail: books@obrien.ie
Website: www.obrien.ie
Reprinted 2001, 2005, 2009, 2010.

ISBN: 978-0-86278-602-1

British Library Cataloguing-in-Publication Data
Colfer, Eoin
Going potty
1.Children's stories
I.Title
823.9'14[J]

5 6 7 8 9 10
10 11 12

The O'Brien Press receives
assistance from

the arts
council
an chomhairle
ealaíon

Editing, typesetting, layout, design: The O'Brien Press Ltd.
Illustrations: Woody
Printed in Germany by Bercker.
The paper in this book is produced using pulp from managed
forests.

CHAPTER 1

Gran's

For his seventh birthday, Ed Cooper's Gran made him a train from egg boxes.

An egg-box train doesn't sound very exciting. But Ed's Gran was an artist. She could make **brilliant** models from the stuff people throw away.

Ed loved the egg-box train. He drove his train through the kitchen, down the hall and along the cracks in the yard. It was his **favourite** thing. Not bad for a piece of cardboard.

One day, Ed forgot to put his
train away. He left it outside. The
rain came down and turned his
train into a soggy **lump**. Ed was
very upset.

He went to ask Gran if there was
anything else to play with. Gran was
busy making a metal **tyrannosaurus**.

Ed nodded and giggled because Gran had some lettuce leaves on her hat, and a **caterpillar** was crawling across her head.

Gran tapped her head. The caterpillar got an awful fright.

Ouch!

TAP TAP

Everything can be a toy, Ed. If you use what's up here.

'Take this, for example,' Gran pulled a potty from the bottom drawer. 'This could be a racing car, or a train-driver's hat,

or even a ship's porthole.'

Ed was surprised. He'd used the potty before, but never as a **toy**.

'You see what games you can invent,' said Gran. 'And I'll finish this dinosaur.'

Ed dragged the potty into the yard and stared at it.

After a while, he realised that the potty **was** like a big toy.

Ed was like his Gran. He had a great imagination.

Ed stayed out in the yard all morning. He had so much fun pretending to be a cowboy or a spaceman, that he forgot all about his egg-box train.

CHAPTER 2

The Potty's Story

One night on a sleep-over, Gran told him the story of the potty.

They snuggled up on the bed together with the potty beside them. This was a **special** treat, because usually the potty wasn't allowed on the bed. But tonight Gran had cleaned it specially.

'A long time ago we bought the potty for your **Great Uncle Pat**. He loved that potty nearly as much as you do. Whenever he wouldn't sleep, we'd sit him on that potty, and he'd nod right off.'

Ed laughed. Imagine Great Uncle Pat on a potty!

'The year after, the **War** started. We lived in London then.'

Ed nodded. He'd heard about the War.

'Every night, big planes would bomb the city. If the **bombs** got too close, my father would take us down into the railway tunnel.

'One night we were all down there, in our pyjamas. We were singing Christmas carols to cheer ourselves up, when the bombs came **really** close.

'A big rock fell from the roof of
the tunnel and clattered poor Pat
right on the **head**.

'Luckily for him, he had the potty on his head, playing soldiers. So it was the potty that took the blow. Cracked clear in **two** it did. Pat hadn't a scratch on him. Although he couldn't hear so well for a few days.'

BONK!

'What about the potty, Gran?'

'Well, the potty was a **hero**, wasn't it? My father stuck it back together, and I got the job of repainting its flowers. After all, it saved Pat's life.'

Gran put on her glasses.

'Let me see ... There, look!'

Ed traced the crack she was pointing at. It ran all the way around the bowl.

'Exactly,' said Gran. 'And that's why no one in this house minds people wearing **potties** on their heads.'

She kissed Ed and tucked him in tight. Wouldn't it be great? thought Ed. Sitting in a tunnel in your pee jays, singing carols and wearing a potty on your head.

CHAPTER 3

Down the Corridor

After the holidays, Ed had to go back to school. Usually Ed liked school.

But this year was different. When you went into first class, **everything** changed.

No more playing in the junior yard with the jungle gym and hopscotch squares. No more home time before the big children.

And worst of all, no more using the special toilets in the infants' room. Now that you were seven, it was down the corridor and into the **big boys' toilet**.

At the school, Ed climbed out of the car. He had a plan. His plan was **not** to go to the toilet until he got home.

By the end of mathematics, Ed knew this plan wasn't going to work. A little pain in his belly was telling him to go to the toilet – and **fast**!

Ed raised his hand and waved it too, so the teacher would know he had to see her **right** now!

Ed felt his face going red.

'I need to ...'

But that was all he could say. It was no good, his lips had closed tight.

Quickly Ed wrote a **message** for the teacher.

'Okay, Ed,' Miss Byrne whispered. 'You can go. Next time just wink twice like this.'

'Like a **code**?' said Ed.

'That's right. Like a code.'

Ed walked down the corridor to
the **boys' toilet**. It was blue and
covered with tiles, like a
swimming pool.

Ed held his breath and pretended he was diving into the water. This wasn't so bad, he thought. He could make the toilets into a **game** too.

There was no one inside, and no noise except the gurgle of water.

'Hello,' said Ed to himself in
the mirror, and gave himself a
little wave. **Mirror Ed** waved
back.

Then the pain in Ed's belly reminded him why he was here, and he went in to the cubicle.

There was a lock on the door, but the catch was missing. This worried Ed, because **someone** could come in.

The toilet itself was **big**.

There could be a frog living in there. Ed shivered. He didn't like frogs that he couldn't see.

Then Ed heard footsteps in the hall.
He imagined **shoes** banging down
the corridor on their own, with legs
sticking out of them, and no boys on
top of the legs.

But there were **boys**. They
were talking and laughing.
They're coming in here, thought
Ed. In to this very cubicle!

Suddenly Ed didn't want to go
to the toilet anymore.

Taking a deep breath, Ed threw open the door and ran out of the big boys' toilet. He didn't even stop to say goodbye to Mirror Ed on the way past. He was **never** coming back. **Never, never, never**!

He would just have to hold on until he got home...

CHAPTER 4

Tell Gran

Holding on until Ed got home was a **big** problem – especially after lunch.

Ed wished that he could take the potty to school, so he wouldn't get pains in his tummy.

One day Miss Byrne asked Ed a question.

'Ed?' she asked. 'Can you spell "ambulance"?'

But Ed could only think about **one** thing these days.

'**Potty!**' he shouted at the top of his voice.

Miss Byrne blinked. 'Pardon, Ed?'

Majella Dempsey stood up, even though you're supposed to get permission.

The whole class laughed then, and Miss Byrne had to tinkle her **Quiet Bell** before they calmed down.

Ed felt **terrible**.

'What *did* you say, Ed?'

Ed could feel his face going red.

He *had* said potty. But he couldn't say it *again*. Not with everybody listening.

If only he could think of a word that rhymed with potty, then he could pretend he'd said that. But all he could think of was **botty**. And that was worse than potty!

Lucky for Ed the bell for **home time** rang.

After school he ran  straight out to the car without even stopping to talk to his friends.

Later in Gran's, Ed was
thinking about how the potty had
saved Uncle Pat.

He touched the
potty. It felt smooth
under his finger.
Maybe, he thought ...

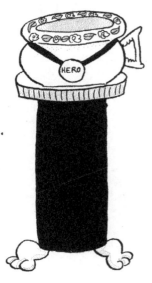

'Gran?' he asked

'Yes, Ed.'

Gran laughed. 'Maybe. If you have a potty kind of a problem.'

Ed's cheeks turned bright **red**
again. He didn't like talking
about the toilet. Not to anyone.

So Ed began to write his story
down. By the time he was finished, Ed
had written **four** full pages.
He handed them
to Gran.

Gran put on her glasses and began to read. Ed looked up at her to see if she was laughing. She wasn't. Gran was reading very **carefully**.

'Do you know what, Ed?' she said at last. 'I think that maybe the potty can help you after all.'

CHAPTER 5

Potty in Disguise

On Monday Ed had to go back to
school. He was hoping that it would
snow and he could stay home. But it
didn't snow. The sun shone
in a clear sky like a big **blob**
of orange paint.

Miss Byrne was waiting for Ed
at the classroom door.

His teacher knelt down so her
face was beside Ed's.

'A little birdie tells me that you
don't like using the **big boys'
toilet**.'

Ed just knew his face was going red.

'Well now,' said Miss Byrne, 'I think we'll have to do something about that.'

She took Ed's hand and led him down the corridor.

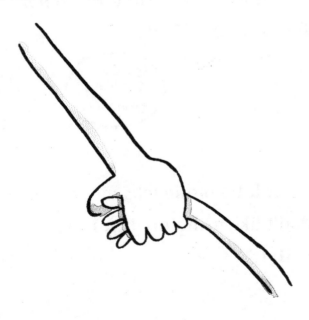

Ed knew where they were going. Oh, no! Miss Byrne was going to bring him into the toilet. Just like an **infant**!

But Miss Byrne stopped at the door.

'Now Ed,' she said. 'I want you to go in.'

Ed shook his head. He didn't want to.

'Don't worry, Ed. Everything will be all right. Use the cubicle in the middle. I think there's a **surprise** for you in there.'

So Ed went in. He looked around to check he was on his own. There was only him and the Ed in the mirror.

The Mirror Ed looked scared. But he couldn't run away. Miss Byrne was watching him.

Ed pushed open the cubicle door and stepped inside.

The first thing he noticed was a new **catch** on the door. Now he could lock the big boys out. This made him feel much better.

There was still the toilet though, and maybe a **frog** inside it.

Then Ed saw his surprise. Someone had painted **flowers** all around the rim of the toilet. Lovely colourful flowers just like on Gran's potty. It was as though the potty was disguised as a school toilet, just for him.

Ed climbed up on the toilet. He could feel the flowers under his fingers. He wasn't one bit afraid anymore. This was like being at Gran's. The potty had **saved** him – like Gran said it would.

After school,
Ed went to visit
Gran. Ed ran into
the kitchen. The
wind chimes
sang when he
opened the door.

'Gran, Gran!'
he shouted. 'You'll **never** guess!'

'Guess what, Ed?'

'The potty!' panted Ed. 'The potty
saved me ...'

But then he stopped. Who had painted flowers on the potty when it broke in two? **Gran** had.

Gran winked at Ed. 'What flowers?'

Ed knew that she was joking because of the smile on her face, and because of the jar of paintbrushes, sitting in rainbow water.

Ed ran and gave his grandmother a big hug.

'**Thanks**, Gran,' he said.

Gran brushed her grandson's hair back with her fingers.

'You're **welcome**, Ed,' she whispered.